In the park there are three stone crocodiles – a big one, a middle-sized one and a small one. In Meera's family there are three children – Alice, Meera and little Mac. One morning, Meera finds Stone Croc, the smallest crocodile, sitting on the doorstep. Mac is delighted. Alice thinks it's wicked. Meera, as usual, has to sort out the problems!

Penelope Farmer has written several fantasy stories for children and young people, such as *A Castle of Bone*, *Thicker than Water* and *Charlotte Sometimes*, which inspired a popular song of the same name by The Cure. Her first published stories were written when she was fifteen and were followed a few years later by her first novel for young people, *Summer Birds*, which was a runner-up for the Carnegie Medal. She is also the author of a number of books for adults, including *Glasshouses*. She is married to a doctor and has two grown-up children.

Other titles to enjoy

Jake's Magic
by Alan Durant

Broops! Down the Chimney
by Nicholas Fisk

Florizella and the Wolves
by Philippa Gregory

Lizzie's List
by Maggie Harrison

Roseanne and the Magic Mirror
by Virginia Ironside

Geoffrey Strangeways
by Jill Murphy

The Magic Skateboard
by Enid Richemont

Change the King!
The Summertime Santa
by Hugh Scott

Harry and Chicken
Harry the Explorer
by Dyan Sheldon

The Wizard in the Woods
Wizard in Wonderland
by Jean Ure

STONE CROC

Penelope Farmer

Illustrations by
Robert Bartelt

WALKER BOOKS
LONDON

For
Perin, Kate and Amy in Bombay
and
Neil and Nick in Alderwasley

(And with apologies, too, to the
children of Ravenscourt Park.
I do know there's only
one stone crocodile, really.)

First published 1991 by Walker Books Ltd
87 Vauxhall Walk, London SE11 5HJ

Text © 1991 Penelope Farmer
Illustrations © 1991 Robert Bartelt

This edition published 1992

Printed and bound in Great Britain by
Richard Clay Ltd, Bungay, Suffolk

British Library Cataloguing Publication Data
Farmer, Penelope
Stone croc.
I. Title
823'.914 [F]
ISBN 0-7445-2070-3

CONTENTS

Chapter One

There were three stone crocodiles in the sandpit in Ravenscourt Park. A big one, a middle-sized one and a little one. Just like the three bears, Meera thought. Just like us, too – Alice and me and Mac.

Of course she didn't expect the smallest crocodile to appear on the doorstep one day. But it did.

Alice was Meera's big sister, grown-up nearly, fourteen years old; a teenager in other words. Mac, short for Macbeth, was their little brother, only three. Meera herself was the middle-sized one, nine years old going on ten. In other families, brothers and sisters were much closer together in age, it seemed to her, close enough to play together. In her family Alice was too old to want to play with Meera, Mac was too young for Meera to play with. On the contrary, she had to look after him. Alice was supposed to help sometimes, but more often than not she said she had a netball practice to go to, or a school disco, or homework to finish, or her hair to dye – orange once, green another time.

Besides, she said, she used to mind Meera, when Meera was little, now it was Meera's turn to mind Mac. "Teenagers," their mother often sighed these days at Alice's doings. So did Meera. I wish *I* was a teenager, she thought sometimes.

Their mother looked
after Mac when Alice
and Meera were at
school, and when
Mac wasn't at
nursery school.
But after school,
she was always in
her room upstairs,
at her sewing machine,
making chair covers to bring in
extra money for their family. The covers
were made of all kinds of material. Some had
birds, some had flowers, some had animals,
some had birds and flowers and animals –
everything you could think of.

"Funny the things people like to sit on,"
Meera's mum said. "It'll be crocodiles next,
I shouldn't wonder."

"Mac likes sitting on the crocodiles in the
sandpit," said Meera.

Their father was a seaman. He sent
postcards from all over the world, from Rio

de Janeiro, Cape Town, Vancouver, Sydney. Sometimes their mother would say, "Your father's going to hear about *this* when he comes home. And then you'll get what for." But they never did get what for, not even Alice. What they got were dolls from Mexico, elephants from Africa, bracelets from India, shells from the South Pacific. Once he bought a wooden crocodile. Mac liked it so much he was allowed to keep it.

"I expect it reminds him of the crocodiles in the sandpit," said Meera. "Mac loves those crocodiles. He'd bring them home if he could."

She was glad he couldn't, though. Crocodiles have such big teeth, she thought. Even the little sandpit crocodile had big teeth. The little crocodile was the one Mac liked best. He didn't just sit on it. He stroked it and banged it with his spade and tipped sandcastles on its head. He rode it like a donkey. Sometimes he lay down flat on top of it and went to sleep.

"That poor stone croc. I wonder it puts up

with you, Mac," said Meera, feeling sorry for it. It was a wonder she put up with Mac herself, come to that. He lay down in the street and screamed. He ran away from her. He threw her paints everywhere, once he cut up her clothes with scissors. Sometimes he kept the whole family awake at night.

"I get a better night's sleep on board ship than I do at home these days, thanks to Macbeth here," Dad said. Macbeth was a man who murdered sleep in a play by Shakespeare. Mac was "Mac" from then on. His real name was John.

The morning
Meera opened
the front door
to get the milk
and found the
little crocodile
sitting on the doorstep
looking at her, sleepily, a bit
like Mac when he had just woken up,
she had no doubt whose fault it was. Now
Mac had murdered its sleep, she thought.
What else could you expect, the way he
tormented the poor stone creature. Why me?
she wondered. Whatever next?

As she was staring at the crocodile, she
heard old Mrs Fisk from the top floor flat
coming down to fetch her milk. Meera
promptly sat on the crocodile. "Enjoying the
sun, dear?" said Mrs Fisk, who was short-
sighted, luckily. "It's a lovely morning, I'll say
that. It'll be summer any day." And she
picked up her milk and went upstairs,
without seeming to have noticed anything.

Meera got to her feet. The crocodile had felt as stonelike as ever to sit on. Perhaps it was stone still, perhaps someone had just put it on their front doorstep for a joke. But as she stared down at it, it heaved itself up, and before she could close the door, followed her inside, and through the hall into her bedroom. It moved very slowly and heavily, it is true, as if it were still stone, rather than anything more lively. On the other hand stone doesn't move, as a rule. Nor does it come looking for someone. Meera assumed the crocodile was looking for Mac. It wouldn't have come to their house otherwise. It must *like* being pestered by Mac, she thought. Maybe it likes being pestered more than I do.

The bedroom she shared with Alice was at the back of the house, behind the living room. The crocodile stared around it suspiciously for a minute, yawned, then slid sideways under Meera's bed. When she picked up the duvet and peered underneath, she found it lying flat just as it did in the park, eyes

closed, seemingly asleep, its mouth smiling as
it always did, its teeth in a line outside its
mouth as they always were.

What big teeth it has, thought Meera.
Hearing her mother call, she pulled the duvet
down carefully to hide the crocodile
completely, and went to have breakfast. She
didn't dare look under her bed again,
afterwards. There was no sound from the
crocodile, so she just put her shoes on, picked
up her day pack and went to school, hoping it
was all a dream. If it wasn't a dream, she
hoped someone else would find the crocodile,
then it would not be her problem any more.
Mac was enough, she thought. She didn't
need a crocodile as well, even a stone one.

* * *

They lived in the middle two floors of a house standing on the far side of the road from Ravenscourt Park, next to the Underground, and just in front of Meera's school. All day you could hear the trains going past, feel them shaking the house, hear the sound of the people playing tennis in the park, the sound of children calling and shouting from the school. Sometimes Meera's class went to play games in the park. They did that day, walking in a class crocodile, two by two, past the sandpit crocodiles. There were, as Meera expected, only two crocodiles left now. She

heard the mothers of little children who used to play with Mac sometimes, talking.

"Someone must have stolen it," Mrs Biggar was saying. "Well, it couldn't have walked, could it?" replied Mrs Scott.

Fat lot you know, Mrs Scott, thought Meera. I wish I didn't know anything, she thought when she got home and looked under the bed to find the crocodile still lying there. It opened its eyes and looked at her. It also opened its mouth very wide, showing all its teeth. It looked hungry. It probably is hungry, she decided. Her mother was calling down from upstairs. "Is that you, Meera, will you give Mac his tea? It's all ready."

Mac had fish fingers and baked beans for his tea. So did the crocodile. There wasn't anything else to give him. Meera wondered how she was going to explain the disappearance of her and Alice's tea too – a large packet of fish fingers and a whole tin of baked beans. Though Mac had a big appetite for a little boy, it wasn't that big.

The crocodile's was, though.

"What are you doing, Meera?" said Alice, seeing Meera hurrying into the bedroom with another plateful. "Feeding a crocodile," said Meera.

"Oh. Wow. I see what you mean," said Alice, when Meera lifted up the duvet cover to show the crocodile chomping up fish fingers, baked bean juice oozing over its pointed teeth and green stone gums. "Wicked," she added. "Just wicked. Where did it come from?"

"It's one of the park crocodiles, of course. How are we going to get it back there?" said Meera.

"Why try to get it back there?" argued Alice.

Neither of them noticed that Mac had climbed down from the table in the living room and followed them into their bedroom.

"My croc," he shouted when he saw the crocodile, hurling himself at it before Meera could stop him. "It's my croc." He didn't seem at all alarmed about its teeth, unlike Meera. He pummelled it and rode on it, and lay on it, just as he did in the park. Not that the crocodile seemed to mind. It even seemed to like it. It kept its teeth for the remains of the fish fingers. Meera stopped worrying, mostly. Alice had not appeared worried in the first place.

"I mean why not keep it? We haven't got a dog or a cat, after all," she insisted.

"Who's going to look after it, then?" asked Meera.

"We are, of course," said Alice. "Just like we look after Mac."

We? Me, most likely, Meera thought. *Teenagers,* Meera sighed to herself.

Chapter Two

As crocodiles went, Meera thought, it was quite a pretty crocodile. It was made of a greenish stone – Alice said it mightn't be stone at all, it might be some kind of metal. But Meera still thought of it as stone: Stone Croc. It was most green on the bits that had got rubbed by children climbing over it; the top of its head, its two big nostrils, its teeth, the hoods of its eyes, the edges of its scales. Apart from being made of metal or stone it was very like a real crocodile, she thought, with its smiling jaws and sleepy eyelids. But in spite of its real-looking teeth it did not seem interested, like real crocodiles, in eating people. What it liked eating most, was what Mac liked eating most. Crisps and ice-cream, sausages and chocolate biscuits. It was not surprising, Alice said, since little children ate things like crisps and ice-cream all over it, all the time. It must have got to like the smell, she said.

The trouble was finding enough crisps and so forth to go round both Mac and the crocodile. Like Mac, Stone Croc was always hungry. They could not go on feeding it on Mac's food – there wasn't enough of Mac's food. Their mother would have started getting suspicious. They had to buy it specially.

"It would be cheaper if Stone Croc ate people. People would come free," said Alice, crossly. That first week, all her paper round money, most of her Saturday job money, as well as her and Meera's pocket-money went on feeding Stone Croc. Because she spent so much more money on the crocodile than Meera did, she said Meera could make up for it by looking after the crocodile. And Mac, of course.

Just what I'd expected anyway, said Meera to herself, as Alice disappeared to sports practice or a school club or to do her homework. Or, one afternoon, to dye her hair again – pink this time – at her friend's house. Luckily Stone Croc was not too much trouble to look after in the beginning. In fact he – Meera thought of Stone Croc as he by now, mostly because of Mac – made Mac easier to mind. He and Mac played together all the time. Meera could even sit in her room and read a book sometimes while Mac and Stone Croc knocked a ball around the floor. She

had never been able to read a book while minding Mac before. When she and Mac went out, Stone Croc slept soundly under her bed. "He's much less trouble than Mac," Alice said. "How do you know?" asked Meera, looking at her pink hair. But it was true, all the same.

She was always afraid, of course, that her mother was going to find out about Stone Croc. He and Mac did not play together quietly. Twice Mr Gatting from the basement flat came up to complain about the sound of Stone Croc's stone legs and belly thumping on the floor. But Mr Gatting was always complaining about something. Moreover the constant sound of her sewing machine meant Meera's mum never heard anything herself. Alice said she wouldn't hear if the house burnt down around her. "It wouldn't burn down if I was there to dial 999," said Meera.

Meera's worst anxiety was looking under the bed every day when she came in from school, in case Stone Croc had got out

somewhere. Her second worst anxiety was
when she had to take Mac to the park. Mac
liked playing on the bigger crocodiles in the
sandpit, now that the little Stone Croc lived
under Meera's bed. Meera imagined those
two much bigger crocodiles turning up on her
doorstep. If they did it would be her who
would have to deal with them, for sure. Her
mum would be too busy sewing, Alice too
busy being a teenager.

"Oh no you don't," she said, the moment
Mac climbed on to the biggest crocodile, and
she dragged him off to the swings. Next time
it was easier to take him away from the
sandpit because they had filled up the
paddling pool with water. Even Mac liked
water better than sand.

"Stone Croc likes water," he said. "Want to bring Stone Croc."

"Oh no you don't," said Meera, turning pale at the thought. "Stone Croc would hate water. He'd melt like ice-cream. Then you wouldn't have him to play with any more."

"Would," said Mac. "Want Stone Croc." He was always talking about Stone Croc these days. But their mother thought he was talking about the sandpit crocodiles. Of course she would, thought Meera. No one – no grown-up at least – would ever guess Stone Croc had walked to their house. His disappearance remained a mystery to everyone. To everyone except Meera and Alice and Mac, that is.

One day Meera's worst fear was realized. She came home from school and found no Stone Croc under the bed.

He wasn't anywhere in her bedroom. He wasn't in the kitchen or in the living room. Anxiously Meera went upstairs and looked in the bathroom. She looked in at the door of the bedroom, where her mother was sewing away as usual, clackety-whirr on her old sewing machine. She was making pink covers this time, with parrots all over them. Her back to the door, she didn't see or hear Meera come in. There was parrot-covered cloth strewn all over the chair and bed; Meera picked up corners of cloth to peer underneath.

"What are you doing, Meera?" asked her mother, turning crossly all of a sudden, taking pins out of her mouth.

"Looking for a crocodile," said Meera, deciding honesty was the best policy.

"Oh, *Meera*. You're as bad as Mac. Go away and stop being silly. I've promised to have this ready by tomorrow," said Mum.

Meera went away. Between chair-cover makers and teenagers and naughty little boys, there was no one except her to look after anything. It's not fair. I'm not even ten yet, she thought.

Mac was sitting on the floor of his back

bedroom where she had left him, saying over and over, "Where's Stone Croc?"

"I wish I knew," Meera started to say. But then suddenly from overhead, from Mrs Fisk's flat, she heard a strange thumping noise. Thumping noises like that didn't usually come from Mrs Fisk's flat. Mrs Fisk was very little and light. She tiptoed about. But this wasn't the sound of anyone tiptoeing. Far from it.

A train went past, shaking the house as usual. For a moment if there were any more thumps overhead, Meera couldn't hear them.

But a moment after she did. And so did Mac.

"Stone Croc," he shouted. Before she could stop him he was out of the door and up the stairs to Mrs Fisk's flat. He often went up there. Mrs Fisk gave him sweets, and said he was a lovely little boy and no trouble. Nor was he ever any trouble with Mrs Fisk. It's not fair, thought Meera.

Today he ran straight into the door of Mrs Fisk's sitting room and there she was as usual sitting by her empty grate, drinking a cup of tea. On the hearth rug in front of her was Stone Croc, noisily lapping up tea from a saucer.

"My Croc," Mac shouted.

"I gave him tea with milk in it, first," said Mrs Fisk. "He didn't like that, but he loves it with sugar in." Meera wondered if she ought to point out that Stone Croc was drinking so greedily he'd slopped tea all over the carpet.

Mrs Fisk might be short-sighted, but the careful way she was watching him, surely she noticed Stone Croc slopping. Maybe she didn't. Or maybe if she did she didn't mind.

While Meera was also wondering whether to point out to Mrs Fisk she was having a crocodile to tea (maybe Mrs Fisk wouldn't mind that either) Mrs Fisk asked, "What sort of doggie is he, then? He looks a bit like a sausage dog to me, a dachshund. Only bigger."

"Stone Croc! Stone Croc!" Mac was yelling still, practically drinking tea out of the saucer alongside Stone Croc.

"He's more like a crocodile dog, really," said Meera cautiously.

"He does seem very hungry. Do you think he's a stray?" Mrs Fisk was asking. "I didn't have any dog food, of course, but I had a tin of cat food left over from Kitty. I gave him that, he ate the whole tin." Kitty was Mrs Fisk's cat. Or had been, before she got run over.

I bet cat food's cheaper than crisps and fish

fingers, Meera was thinking. I must tell Alice. Lucky Mrs Fisk's so short-sighted, she was also thinking.

"Can we take our crocodile home again?" she asked very politely.

"Is that his name, Crocodile?" asked Mrs Fisk.

"No, he is a crocodile," said Meera.

"Good doggie," said Mrs Fisk. "Like a sweetie for being a good boy, Mac?"

"Thank you for the cat food. Come on home now, Mac," said Meera. Now what? Where will Stone Croc get to next, she was wondering. Looking at Stone Croc thumping downstairs ahead of her, she suspected that the quiet time was over. That this was only the beginning of her problems. And she was right.

Chapter Three

Stone Croc went up to see Mrs Fisk quite often after that. She bought him dog food specially. She called him Crockie.

"Oh how I miss Kitty," she said. "I like having Crockie around. He isn't any trouble. But my, isn't he hungry?"

It meant less of Alice's paper round money went on feeding Stone Croc. But it didn't mean Alice spent more time minding him and Mac. Meera still did that. She was at her wits' end quite soon.

One day she went into her bedroom to find that Mac had climbed on Stone Croc's back and reached her poster paints again. He had also managed to reach the tap in the kitchen. There were red, blue and green Stone Croc pawmarks all over the floor and the beds. There were red, blue and green Mac handprints all over the beds and up the walls. Meera smacked Mac, the way her mother did sometimes. She also smacked Stone Croc. But she didn't hurt either of them. She just gave herself a sore hand. The next minute Mac was lying on his back kicking his heels and screaming, the first tantrum he'd had since Stone Croc came.

Stone Croc, after watching for a moment with an interested look, also lay down on his back and kicked his paws. He didn't scream, though. He couldn't. But he did make little grunts as if he were trying to. Meera had never heard him make any sound before. His kicking paws, on the other hand, made much more noise than Mac's feet. Between that and the screams, Mr Gatting was upstairs complaining in two minutes.

Meera had to run down to the shop to spend what was left of her pocket-money on a packet of Maltesers to quieten them both. Then she had run upstairs to tell her mother about Mac's tantrum, and pass the message on from Mr Gatting. Her mother was working on blue stuff covered in striped orange elephants. Horrid, thought Meera.

"Funny the things people want to sit on," said her mother, laughing. "That Mac. That Mr Gatting," she said, shaking her head.

Two nights later Stone Croc woke up in the middle of the night and wouldn't go back to sleep. He danced on the floor. He woke up Mr Gatting as well as Meera and Alice. Next morning Mr Gatting came up and complained again.

That wasn't Mac's fault, of course. But their mother thought it was Meera and Alice's fault. She wasn't laughing any more. She stopped their pocket-money this time, anyway. Perhaps she'd also stopped thinking striped elephants were funny.

Three days later, just before Mac's bedtime, he and Stone Croc between them managed to open the kitchen door and escape down the back steps into Mr Gatting's garden.

Mr Gatting was very proud of his garden. He grew bushes on one side, vegetables on the other and flowers in the middle. He had a patch of lawn just big enough for the deck chair which he set out every sunny summer Sunday and sat on all afternoon reading his newspaper. In one corner he had built a barbecue out of bricks and a boot scraper. On fine evenings he grilled sausages and steaks, tomatoes and mushrooms on the barbecue for his tea. The smell would float up through their kitchen windows making them all feel hungry.

Mr Gatting was a tubby man. Obviously he liked his food. Obviously he liked his food better than he liked people. For he never invited them to eat the sausages with him. He never invited anyone. Meera's mother said he was the loneliest man she'd ever come across. Apart from going to the pub sometimes with Meera's dad when he came home, he always went out alone. And then Meera's mum would sigh and say she wished they had a garden. It would be so good for Mac to be able to play outside in a garden.

But Mac was playing out in the garden, now. Out of the window Meera could see his arms full of flowers from Mr Gatting's border. Stone Croc stood in the next bed with a mouthful of carrot tops and pea pods. By the time she had got downstairs and out into

-34-

the garden, however, Mac had dropped the
flowers and Stone Croc the carrot tops. They
had found the barbecue instead. They had
also found the remains of Mr Gatting's tea.
Stone Croc was eating cold sausages. Mac
had tipped out what looked like a whole
bottle of tomato ketchup on to a plate and
was slurping it up with his fingers. As Meera
came round the corner of the house he
offered the plate to Stone Croc. Eagerly Stone
Croc dipped in his snout. When he lifted his
head, ketchup was dripping off it.

At that very moment Mr Gatting arrived.
He had an apron on and a tea-cloth in one
hand. He must be doing the washing
up, thought Meera. She also
noticed he was wearing a
ketchup-coloured tie.

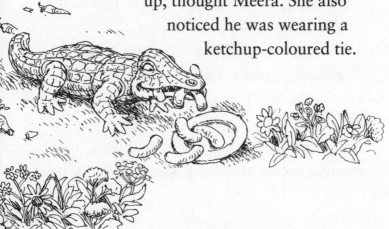

"Will you get that animal out of here!" he shouted, charging at Stone Croc whose crocodile grin looked more interesting than ever, now it was dripping red. He might really have been eating people this time, thought Meera. Mac had found another sausage and was biting into it. He took no notice of Mr Gatting. When Meera made a grab at his hand, he twisted out of the way, laughing excitedly.

Mr Gatting raised a short leg and brown-shoed foot to kick Stone Croc. Then he paused. He looked more closely at Stone Croc. His voice, which had been shouting, grew quiet.

"What kind of animal is that?" he asked.

"It's a crocodile," said Meera.

"Whatever it is," he said testily, "would you mind getting it out of my garden. I'll have some words with your mother about this."

But he took his foot back, as if he had thought better of kicking Stone Croc. Or of

getting near him altogether. It seemed to
Meera that Mr Gatting was definitely edging
away a bit.

"Funny kinds of dogs they breed these
days," he said. Turning to Mac, he said,

"Little boy, do you know what a thief is?
T – H – I – E – F? That's my sausage you're
eating."

Mac went on eating the sausage. He even
dipped one end in tomato sauce. He smiled at
Mr Gatting, an angelic if ketchuppy smile,
Meera thought. Mac could look like an angel
sometimes, especially when he was asleep.
Mr Gatting did not think Mac looked like an
angel. Seeing his face turn almost the same
colour as his tie and as Mac's smile, Meera
said hastily, "Come here at once, Mac," and
grabbed him by the hand. As she did so she
kicked away the flowers that Mac had
dropped, blue delphiniums, red poppies, a
crimson lupin. She hoped that Mr Gatting
would not notice them. At least not yet, not
till she and Mac and Stone Croc were safely
back in the flat.

She nudged Stone Croc with her foot. Stone
Croc snuffled at it affectionately, putting
ketchup stains on her toes. But then to her
surprise he started trotting obediently round

the house and back up the steps to their kitchen. Mac pulled at her hand for a minute, before he, too, followed Meera and Stone Croc. Behind them Mr Gatting had regained his voice – waving the ketchup bottle in one hand, the blue-striped tea-towel in the other – he was looking after them shouting, exactly what Meera could not hear. She did not need to hear to know what he meant.

Sure enough, while she was bathing Mac, the doorbell rang. Mum answered it. Ten minutes later she was back.

"Really, Meera. I'm already behind with the elephant order. Now I've had Mr Gatting shouting at me for ten minutes. Can't I leave Mac with you for five minutes without him

getting into trouble? And what's all this nonsense about a crocodile? Or a dog? Really, I couldn't make head or tail of it. Your dad's going to hear about this. And he's going to give you what for. Crocodiles, indeed!"

There was a lot more about flowers and ketchup and sausages and so forth. As far as Meera could make out she was not going to have any pocket-money for a year by the time it had all been paid for. Mac was too young to get pocket-money, so it couldn't come out of his. And of course it wasn't Alice's fault. Alice, as usual, hadn't been there. She'd been doing her homework round at her friend's house. She arrived home at that moment. She must have been doing her hair as well as her homework, thought Meera, looking at the unfamiliar black ribbon in her still-pink hair.

"It's your turn, Alice. You've got to think of something. Mac is one thing, a crocodile is too much."

"There's lots of stone animals at the Natural History Museum," said Alice. "Why don't we take him there? That's what I've been thinking. Stone Croc might like it there."

"He likes it *here*," said Meera. "That's the whole trouble."

Alice looked at Stone Croc who was lying asleep under the bed, smiling as usual. "Crocodiles always look as if they're smiling," she said.

"Not the way Stone Croc does," said Meera. "Stone Croc's different."

Chapter Four

Meera couldn't sleep that night. She heard the last train stopping at Ravenscourt Park station. She did not remember if she slept then, maybe she did. Yet still she heard the first train in the morning, the one that hooted, then rushed through the station without stopping. And then she heard the heavier sound of the yellow train that didn't carry passengers but looked after the tracks.

She thought of what it would be like taking Stone Croc on the Underground. Alice hadn't seemed a bit worried.

"We could dress him in a dog jacket," she'd said, "to look like a dog." Meera wondered how they would pay for a dog jacket. Or even find one to buy for that matter. There was no pet shop very near. She didn't think that a dog jacket would make Stone Croc look like a dog. Perhaps it didn't matter. It hadn't mattered with Mrs Fisk and Mr Gatting.

In the morning Alice thought better of the dog jacket. "One of Mac's sweaters might be better," she said. But Mac's sweaters weren't big enough. In the end he had to have one of Meera's, her favourite red sweater with little pigs all over it. "All my sweaters would be too big," said Alice. Of course, thought Meera.

Framed by the red wool of the sweater, Stone Croc's bulging eyes and big nostrils, his smiling mouth edged with teeth, didn't look

−43−

the least as if they belonged to a dog. He looked like a crocodile in a sweater with pigs all over it. Alice put Mac's woolly hat on his head. He still looked like a crocodile so she took it off. Instead she made him a collar out of an old belt of their mother's. Meera made a lead out of Alice's school scarf.

Their mother was sewing another set of covers now, green ones patterned with fishes. She seemed to have forgotten about the trouble with Mr Gatting. When Alice suggested taking Meera and Mac to the Natural History Museum, she gave them their fares and entrance money and a bit over for ice-cream without them even having to ask for the ice-cream money. She had been paid extra for the striped elephant covers, she said. Meera deserved a treat for looking after Mac.

"Mac 'serves treat too," said Mac, who was wearing an old pair of dark glasses with bright pink rims that Mrs Fisk had given him.

"You are having a treat. You're going to see the dinosaurs," said Alice.

"Want to see dinosaurs," said Mac.

"I'm not taking him anywhere wearing those," said Alice. But when Meera tried to take the spectacles away from Mac, he screamed so loudly that Alice said, "OK, OK, I give up. If Mac wants to look a freak that's his problem."

"The glasses go nicely with your pink hair, Alice," said Meera.

"Want to see dinosaurs," said Mac.

They could hear their mother's sewing machine through her open window as they set off. Meera thought she could still hear it humming when they stood on the station platform. But maybe it was only trains a long way off. The man at the ticket office gave Stone Croc a funny look. He made them buy a dog ticket for him, which took most of the ice-cream money. They had just missed one train. They reached the platform to find it empty except for themselves. Meera was thankful, what with the pink hair, the pink spectacles, the pig-covered sweater and so forth. Not to mention the way Mac and Stone Croc were behaving.

Stone Croc kept running up and down the edge of the platform peering at the line. Every now and then he gave a little leap as if he wanted to jump down on to it. Meera could not hold him. Alice had her hands full with Mac, who was trying to climb on to the railings above the steps one minute, the next running to the edge of the platform alongside Stone Croc looking for trains. His pink

spectacles fell off all the time. He kept stopping to put them on again. Once they almost fell on to the line. Meera thought, any minute now, he'd be climbing down on the line to fetch them. Fortunately another train arrived at that moment.

In the train Alice and Meera sat side by side, and tried to persuade Stone Croc to sit as close under their feet as possible. But he was very restless. Almost as restless as Mac, who stood up on the seat looking out of the window, putting his spectacles on and taking them off again.

Stone Croc twitched his tail. He poked his snout out from behind their legs. Once it caught the bare ankles of a woman in red sandals standing just behind him, holding on to the train strap above their heads. She looked down to see what had touched her. Immediately she gave a little shriek.

"Isn't that a crocodile?" she asked, faintly.

"'S'my Stone Croc," insisted Mac, looking round from the window.

"He's our dog really," said Alice.

"A sort of dachshund," added Meera, hurriedly, remembering what Mrs Fisk had said.

"He doesn't bite," said Alice.

"I should hope not," said the red-sandalled woman, moving away.

"Want to see dinosaurs," said Mac.

"By the look of it, everyone thinks we're bringing our dinosaurs with us," said Alice.

For other people were staring at Stone Croc now. When they weren't staring at Stone Croc, they were staring at Alice's pink hair. When they weren't looking at either of them they were staring at Mac bouncing up and down on his seat wearing his pink spectacles.

"Rum pets some people keep these days," Meera heard someone say. "Did she say it was a dog?" muttered a fat man in checked shorts. "Looks more like a crocodile to me."

"Got a good set of teeth on him, hasn't he," said a young man in a striped rugger shirt, sitting on the seat opposite. "A friend of mine kept pythons once. They were man-eaters, all right. Or could have been. Not that they had any teeth. They just squeezed you to death, then ate you, if you let them."

At that moment, as it happened, Meera wouldn't have minded a few pythons around, if not to squeeze Stone Croc or Mac to death precisely, at least to hold them still for one moment. Mac had got tired of looking out of the window. He wanted to run up and down the carriage. So did Stone Croc. It took all four of Alice's and Meera's hands, and all four of their feet too to keep Stone Croc sitting underneath them. There was not much they could do about Mac.

Stone Croc was getting more and more annoyed, it seemed to Meera. Rumbling through his body she could feel if not hear, what would have been furious little snorts and squeaks if he'd made them aloud. She wondered if he could bite her hand off if he wanted, with his fine set of teeth. At the same time she began to be afraid he'd lie down soon and have a tantrum, just like Mac.

Fortunately the train stopped then, at the museum station. Alice grabbed Mac, Meera tugged Stone Croc's lead and out they got, safe and sound, all except for Mac's pink spectacles which fell off on the train step. Before they could pick them up again the door closed, the train gave a grunt, a jerk, and left.

Mac had a tantrum then. He lay down
on the platform and screamed very loudly.
Not that Meera could do anything about it.
Stone Croc seemed so anxious to get to the
museum, or so glad to get out of the train,
he'd run away with her by then, up the steps,
past the ticket-collector and into the long
tunnel which led to the museum.

All the way down the tunnel he ran,
dodging astonished people – Meera didn't
know how she managed not to run into some
of them, or tangle them up in Stone Croc's
lead. As it was, a woman in a yellow sun hat

almost fell over, just from surprise. Past the steps that led to the museum they went, right to where the tunnel ended. Stone Croc stopped dead then, and sat down as if he'd worn himself out. Meera had to drag him all the way back down the echoing tunnel. He really felt like stone now. By the time they reached the museum steps, Alice had arrived there with Mac, who wasn't crying any longer.

"I told him the dinosaurs would be frightened if they saw his pink spectacles," said Alice.

"Mac wants to see dinosaurs," said Mac.

At the top of the steps, they found themselves inside the museum railings. The grey-blue museum building towering over their heads had stone carvings from top to bottom. Close to, most of the carvings were of animals, just as Alice said. Meera saw birds; a monkey with long tail and sorrowful eyes. The nearest thing to Stone Croc she saw, though, was a lizard.

"Let's see what they've got inside," said Alice.

"Going to see dinosaurs now?" asked Mac.

Just inside the big swing doors however, two uniformed men were standing at a table examining people's bags and handbags, to make sure they weren't carrying guns or bombs.

One of them noticed Stone Croc.

"No dogs in here," he intoned, loudly.

"But he isn't a dog exactly," argued Alice.

"No pets of any kind," said the man, eyeing her pink hair.

"Maybe we could leave him with the coats," said Alice. "Maybe we could leave my little brother with the coats too," she said hopefully. "Stop that, Mac." Mac had started crawling under the table. He was about to untie the shoelaces of one of the man's very shiny shoes, by the look of it.

"Don't be cheeky," said the man to Alice.

At first Meera had been too busy looking at the tall arched ceilings of the museum and at the pillars holding them up, to see what was going on behind them. For there were stone animals twined round every pillar. There were more sorrowful monkeys, more birds, more lizards. She saw a fox and a rat also. But now she suddenly noticed the queue that was building up. She felt very embarrassed.

"Come away, Alice. It doesn't matter," she said. "Come on, Mac. Come on, Stone Croc."

"It does matter," said Alice. "It's not fair to dogs. Or crocodiles," she hissed.

"Want to see dinosaurs," said Mac,

jumping up from under the table and smiling his angel smile at the uniformed men.

The uniformed men didn't seem to think Mac looked any more like an angel than Mr Gatting had. "If you want to see dinosaurs, young man, leave your pets behind," he said.

"'S'not a pet," said Mac. "'S'my Stone Croc."

"There's a dinosaur for you, Mac," said Alice, pointing. "Look, see that big one there? And look, there's a little one in a glass case. Look!"

Meera only just managed to catch Mac then as he started running into the museum towards the dinosaurs. "Want to see dinosaurs," he howled, fighting to get away from her. Looking back, Meera saw that the queue for the uniformed men and the bag search stretched right out now through the glass doors.

"What's going on?" A fat woman was asking. "Get a move on," shouted a thin man in a straw hat. Other people shouted words

Meera didn't understand because they didn't seem to be in English. But from the tone of the voices they must have meant much the same as the things that were said in English.

She felt her face growing redder and redder with embarrassment.

"Come on, Mac, come on, Stone Croc, come on Alice," she pleaded. And in a moment, to her surprise, they did, all three of them.

"Want to see dinosaurs," sobbed Mac, as they stood outside the glass doors again, watching other people go in.

"Don't be silly, Mac," said Alice, "You saw the dinosaurs. I showed them to you. Look," she pointed. "Look, Meera. There's a good place for Stone Croc. You couldn't put him on a pillar, he'd fall off. But he'd look nice sitting on a stone column, like the one at the top of these steps."

"There's another one at the other side of the steps," said Meera. "You'd need another Stone Croc to sit on top of that."

"Let's put Mac on it," said Alice, looking at him. "Leave him behind too."

At that moment Meera would have liked to leave Alice behind as well. She didn't say so. On the other hand, she wasn't sure she wanted to leave Stone Croc behind, after all. But she didn't know what else they were going to do with him.

"Come on, Meera," Alice was urging her. "Help me lift Stone Croc up. See if he likes it."

Stone Croc must have used up most of his energy running up the tunnel. Ever since they

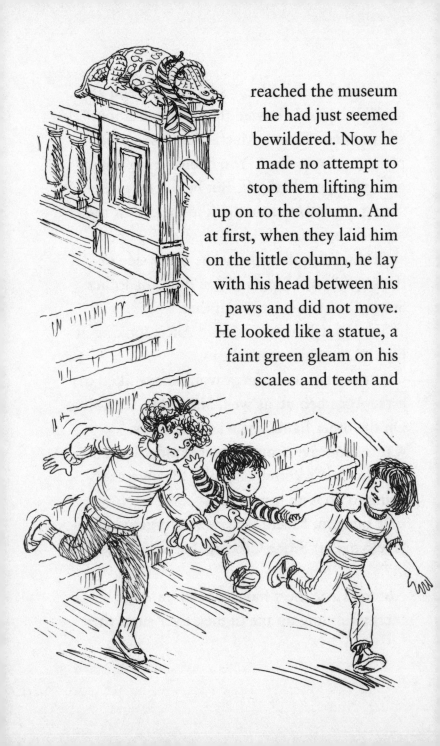

reached the museum
he had just seemed
bewildered. Now he
made no attempt to
stop them lifting him
up on to the column. And
at first, when they laid him
on the little column, he lay
with his head between his
paws and did not move.
He looked like a statue, a
faint green gleam on his
scales and teeth and

nostrils. At least he would have looked like a statue if he had not still been wearing a red sweater covered in little pink pigs.

"What about my sweater?" Meera asked.

"Quick," said Alice, taking no notice. "I think he's turning back to stone again. Quick, Meera. Grab Mac. Run. Quick. Before he notices we're going."

Obediently Meera ran. But Mac had stopped sobbing, "Want dinosaurs." Instead he sobbed, "Stone Croc, Stone Croc," and kept pulling her back. She turned her head after a minute, and saw Stone Croc climbing, slowly, heavily, like a stone crocodile, to his feet.

"Perhaps it's because he's still got my sweater on," she said as Stone Croc lowered himself off the column, and started lumbering after them, watched with astonishment by a newly-arrived group of tourists.

"It's all right Stone Croc, we weren't really leaving you," she panted, as she ran back to meet him. What could they have been thinking of, she wondered. For of course they couldn't have left him behind really, any more than they could have left Mac. Not when it came to it. Not really. To make things worse, Stone Croc seemed quite as unhappy about it as Mac would have been if they tried to leave him. He was crying. Or she thought he must be.

For now was only what – the second or the third time – she heard him making a sound of some kind; little low hoots. It wouldn't have been crying in anyone else, but might have been, in fact most likely was, in a crocodile. In a crocodile baby anyway. Perhaps those other park crocodiles, she thought, weren't Stone Croc's brothers or sisters. Perhaps they were his father and mother.

Alice was kneeling beside Stone Croc petting him. So was Mac.

"Stone Croc sad," he said. "Poor Stone Croc."

"Do you think ice-cream would stop him crying?" asked Alice. "We've got lots of money, not having to pay for the museum."

"It would stop Mac crying," said Meera. "Usually it would." She stayed beside Stone Croc, stroking his stone flank, his stone nostrils, while Alice went to the ice-cream van standing in the street outside. Then all four of them ate vanilla cones with a chocolate flake in the middle, sitting on the museum steps. Stone Croc knocked his out of Meera's hand before long, and snuffled it up off the ground. His little hooting noises had stopped altogether. His smiling jaws looked much as ever, apart from being covered with vanilla and chocolate. Mac's jaws were covered with vanilla and chocolate too. Meera cleaned both of them up, one after the other with an old tissue she found in her jeans pocket.

Chapter Five

Three days later, a week earlier than anyone expected, their father came home on leave. He brought, as he always did, a huge suitcase full of clothes and books and presents. Meera answered the door to him. Other people's fathers put the key in the lock when they came home, she thought. But her father said there was no point in carrying a door key around the world. So his homecoming was announced by the doorbell, not just one ring, though, but two or three, as if he couldn't bear to wait one single second longer to be let into the family again.

He picked Meera up and whirled her

round, bellowing out her name. His big
brown beard tickled her face as it always did;
but she didn't mind. Everyone came running
then, everyone was hugging him and
laughing; Mum was even crying a little. But
later, while they were all having tea, silence
fell – it always did fall sooner or later, when
their father first came home. It was as if no
one knew quite what to say to him after all
this time. As if he did not know quite what to
say to them.

It was worse this time because of Stone Croc. For Meera and Mac and Alice, Stone Croc was more in their minds than anything. Yet they couldn't tell their father about him – at least Alice and Meera couldn't. Mac went on and on and on about "My Stone Croc". Of course their father didn't know what he meant.

"It's just his latest game, this croc thing," their mother said.

The flat seemed much smaller when Dad was around. He was so much bigger than anyone else in the family. He made so much more noise than anyone else, more noise than Mac even. His laugh, his beard, his broad shoulders and long legs filled the hall and the living room and the kitchen. His clothes and packages were all mixed up with the bales of cloth, the packets of pins and buttons and boxes of different coloured threads in their mother's bedroom. Mum didn't do any sewing when their father was at home. At first she smiled all the time, and wore her prettiest clothes. Sometimes she even wore a sari. The whole house smelt different – a smell made up of a mixture of things, not just the good food she cooked, instead of sewing.

It smelt of her father's beard, Meera thought, and the pipe he smoked and of something more foreign, the smell of India or the Far East. Maybe it was the sandalwood soap and sticks of incense, the little bottles of scent that he'd brought home this time. He'd brought lengths of silk, also, to make them clothes, and plaster elephants, and strings of paper birds, and tigers with nodding heads for Mac. Mac broke the birds and tigers and elephants, and then he cried. Their mother said they were too delicate for him. Dad should have brought him something stronger.

They all had much less time to think of
Stone Croc. Stone Croc spent more and more
of the day upstairs with Mrs Fisk. When he
wasn't upstairs he hid under Meera's bed.
They had difficulty in making him come out.

"Anyone would think he was frightened of
Dad," said Alice.

Mac didn't play with him any more, or
hardly ever, only when their father was out
with Mum, and Meera and Alice were
looking after him. Then usually Mac would
be very cross. He would kick Stone Croc and
pull his ears. "Want Daddy," he said. "Horrid
Stone Croc."

If Dad was at home, on the other hand, Mac climbed all over him and shouted in his ears and pulled his hair, much the same way as he treated Stone Croc. At first their father would bellow with laughter and throw him up in the air and say things like "There's my nifty boy." Or, "Isn't he a chip off the old block?"

But as the visit went on he grew angry with Mac sometimes. Mac spilled all his tobacco over the floor once. Another time he tried to pull the gold braid off his sailor's peaked cap. Their father shouted at him. Once he even smacked Mac. Then Mum was cross with Dad, while Mac was cross with Alice and Meera and their mother.

"Won't," he said. "Shan't." "Don't like you." "Daddy, go away." But above all, "Horrid Stone Croc."

"I don't know if Stone Croc's frightened of Dad. I do think he's sad, though," Meera said.

"How can he be sad?" asked Alice. "Look at the way he smiles all the time."

"He can't help smiling," Meera said patiently. "That's the way his face is made. Mrs Fisk thinks he's sad too. She says he's not as hungry as he used to be."

"Perhaps he misses his daddy and mummy," said Alice, joking.

"I wonder if he does," said Meera, not joking. "I wonder if those other crocodiles in the sandpit are his father and his mother."

"Well perhaps you'd better take him back there," said Alice, patting her hair. You could only just see a little pink in it now. Their father had laughed at her, said she looked like a powder puff, he'd seen odd things in his travels but not much odder. She'd look pretty funny in Bangkok, he said.

"Everything in Bangkok would look funny to me," said Alice.

"Don't be cheeky, my girl," Dad said. "I wouldn't let one of my crew talk to me like that."

Next day Alice went round to her friend's after school. When she came back her hair was black and tied with a scarlet ribbon like a little girl's. She had a blue ribbon in it now. Also a yellow and a green ribbon. It was done up all over in little plaits. Meera thought she looked just as strange as she had done with pink hair, but she didn't say so. *Teenagers*, she thought.

"Dad nearly caught Stone Croc today," she said. "He came into our room while I was giving him his tea. He only just got back under the bed in time. Dad asked what I had fish fingers on the floor for. I said I was giving my dolls their tea."

"He's bound to catch him one day," said Alice. "He's not like Mum, he knows everything that's going on."

Meera worried about it more and more. She worried about everything more and more. Above all she worried because Stone Croc looked so sad; his smile made her want to weep, not laugh. His snout reached out further and further, when he lay down. The very hoods of skin over his eyes, over his nostrils, seemed to sag. She even wished he'd make a noise again and bring Mr Gatting up to complain. But he didn't play, he didn't make any noise at all.

She began to wonder about getting him back to the sandpit. But you couldn't make Stone Croc go anywhere he didn't want to go. With Alice's help, she might have been able to, of course. But when Meera suggested it, Alice told her not to be so silly.

"If he wanted to go back there," she said, "he'd've gone long ago. All he has to do is walk out of the front door."

Now that Stone Croc wasn't making a nuisance of himself, Alice didn't seem to worry about him any more. Nor did Mac. Whereas Meera lay awake night after night listening to the trains stop and start, worrying about everything. Somebody had to, she thought.

One evening, to her relief, Stone Croc seemed more cheerful. Mac was playing with him again, chasing an old ball around the room.

"Mr Gatting will be up any moment,"
Meera said to herself, happily. But at that
moment she heard the front door open, and
before she could warn anyone or stop
anything her bedroom door opened also.
There stood her father, filling
up the whole door space
it seemed to her,
staring at them
all. Staring at
Stone Croc.
His hands
were full of
balloons;
the silver
kind that
float into
the air of
their own
accord.

Standing in the doorway, with a whole bunch tugging in his hands he seemed about to fly up to the ceiling, any minute.

"What's that?" he asked. Stone Croc looked frozen to the floor, more like a stone croc than ever. His grin was not sad now, just terrified. Meera wanted to hug him. She did hug him. She had never known him feel so hard. His scales gleamed against her cheek as cold as metal.

"It's my Stone Croc," said Mac.

"Is it now?" said their father. He did not seem surprised at all. But then he must have seen so many much stranger things on his travels, Meera thought. Why ever had she thought her sailor father would be horrified at the sight of Stone Croc?

"Where did you pick him up then?" he was asking, bending down to touch him. Meera felt Stone Croc shrink under her hand. She heard, or thought she heard, a small squeak from him; more like a mouse than a crocodile.

"He just turned up. He seems to like us. He doesn't do any harm," she said.

"Well, he hasn't eaten you all at least. He's obviously not a man-eater," said their father laughing. "But you'd better not tell your mother."

Mac was more interested in the balloons than anything else. "Want one," he said, pointing at one with WHIZZO written on it, in pink writing.

"You can have them all," said Dad.

"Stone Croc wants one too," insisted Mac.

"Then Stone Croc can have one," said Dad, picking a balloon out of the bunch and putting it down beside him. The balloon floated up to the ceiling straight away. Meera thought she could detect Stone Croc's eyes following it. She felt a little less worried suddenly. Stone Croc was beginning to unfreeze beneath her hand. His skin gave a bit, it seemed to her. He felt altogether softer to touch.

Mac and his father were chasing balloons round the floor. As usual, Dad's presence made the room look much smaller; his feet seemed everywhere at once. Stone Croc had gone under the bed to avoid them. On the other hand he was poking his nose out so he could watch. This seemed a good sign to Meera.

Mr Gatting is sure to be up soon, she thought, listening to Mac's shrieks and the thump of Dad's feet and body as he dived for balloons. Not that Mr Gatting seemed to matter now that their father was there. The loud ring on the door bell, five minutes or so later, did not worry her in the least.

Afterwards, Meera could hear the rumble of her father's and Mr Gatting's voices in the hall. But they did not sound angry. And a few minutes later Dad came back into the room and said, "Now then kids, enjoy yourselves, I've told Reg here I'll buy him a pint in the pub, just to make up. Tell your mum will you?"

There were ten days left of their father's leave. He and Mr Gatting went to the pub together most of those nights. Mr Gatting did not cook his supper on his barbecue once in all that time. Meera hoped he felt less lonely now. She did not know about her mother. The balloons had all started to sag, they would not fly up to the ceiling any more. Hardly another word was said about Stone Croc.

On the ninth evening, their father came home from the pub earlier than usual. Mum had cooked a special dinner of chicken and vegetable curry – their father loved curry – and apple pie. Even Mac was allowed to stay up to eat it, though he asked for fish fingers instead of curry.

On the next day, the tenth, their father put

on his uniform and his gold braided cap,
gathered up his large suitcases, told them to
be good while he was gone and kissed them
all goodbye.

"See you don't let that crocodile eat you before I get home," he said, winking at Meera, as he went out of the door. Mum thought he was joking, Meera could see.

That day Meera's mother started on a new set of covers, monkeys this time, climbing palm trees, and the sound of her sewing machine pattered away again in their house. Mac fell over and hurt his knee. Meera got an A at school for a story she wrote. Dad will be pleased, she thought. Then she remembered he wasn't there to tell and wanted to cry for a minute. Alice went round to her friend's house for tea and came back with purple hair.

As for Stone Croc, the very next evening, Meera looked under her bed in the middle of the night and found that he had gone.

Chapter Six

He must be there, she thought. She sat up in
bed and looked around the room. The full
moon flooding through the window made it
almost as bright as daylight, but much more
mysterious. On the floor the scattered clothes,
the box of Mac's toys, the drooping balloons,
made the strangest shapes and shadows. But
there was not one shape which could have
been Stone Croc.

She climbed out of bed and peered under it
again, more carefully, to make sure she hadn't
missed seeing him in a far corner. But he was
not there. He was not under Alice's bed
either. The sleeping Alice did not stir as

Meera crawled about, even though Meera banged against her bed a few times.

Meera shook her awake, at last. "Alice," she hissed. "Alice. Alice. Stone Croc's gone."

"He can't have," said Alice, sitting up crossly, rubbing her eyes. "Go back to sleep, Meera."

"But he has. I can't find him anywhere. And look, the door's open." For it was. Not wide open, she'd have noticed that sooner. But open enough for Stone Croc to have crept out.

"OK, OK." Alice began to take notice now. She even began to get dressed. They both got dressed – that was just as well, because when they went out to the kitchen the door on to the balcony was open too. Their mother did sometimes leave it open on hot nights. When their father was home he told her she shouldn't.

But there was no sign of Stone Croc on the balcony nor on the steps, nor in the whole of Mr Gatting's garden. They searched everywhere; among the heaps of flowerpots he stored beneath their balcony; by the barbecue; under the shrubs along the wall at the back; behind the little shed where he kept his tools and the garden chair on which he sat every fine summer Sunday reading his newspaper.

Alice seemed to Meera to make a lot of noise. She fell over flowerpots, she stubbed her toe on the steps and said "Ouch", very loudly.

"You'll wake Mr Gatting," Meera warned her.

"Bother Mr Gatting. What about Stone Croc? Look, there's a hole in the fence behind the shed – do you think he's got out through there?"

Cautiously, they unbolted the door to the street and crept out. But there was no sign of Stone Croc in the street, either.

"At least he hasn't got run over," said Alice.

"There aren't any cars in the night-time," Meera pointed out.

"Maybe Stone Croc's gone into the park to look for the other two

crocodiles," said Alice, taking no notice.
"Maybe they are his mother and father."

"I said that," said Meera. She didn't expect
Alice to hear.

"Maybe if we go into the park we'll find
three crocodiles in the sandpit again,"
said Alice.

Meera was not sure what she thought about that, after all.

"Cheer up, Meera," said Alice. "You could still go and see him every day, couldn't you? And you won't have to spend all your pocket-money on crisps and dog food. Let's go and have a look."

Though there were holes in the park fence big enough to let through dogs or stone crocs, they weren't big enough for Alice and Meera. They climbed over the park gates instead. Alice helped Meera climb down the other side. Then they ran towards the sandpit.

Meera did not know if it would be a relief to find Stone Croc safe there, or whether it would be sad to see three crocodiles again, instead of two. It would mean Stone Croc never sleeping under her bed again, never chomping up spaghetti or fish fingers, never smiling at Meera what looked to her like a real smile sometimes, not just a crocodile smile, in spite of all the teeth.

"Who will Mac play with now?" she asked.

"You, of course. Just like he always used to. You like playing with Mac. Mum says so," said Alice.

Meera sighed. "Sometimes I like playing with Mac," she said. "Sometimes I don't."

They had come out of the entrance path, could see beyond the trees, the open lawn in the middle of the park. They had almost reached the sandpit. But before they could check how many crocodiles there were, Alice grabbed Meera's arm and said urgently, "Look. Do you see what I'm seeing?"

Of course it could be that their eyes were

playing tricks on them, Meera thought. The silvery-grey light drained colour from everything, nothing looked quite as it normally did. Black shadows were very black and big. The moon space of the lawn seemed to reach for ever.

But Meera did not think her eyes were playing tricks. It really did look like Stone Croc lying in the middle of the grass.

She ran towards him, followed by Alice. At once Stone Croc got to his feet, and waited a little while, looking back at them. But when they were within a few metres of him, he suddenly began to run. It was like the day

they went to the museum, Meera thought. But this time he wasn't on a dog lead, he was free. She couldn't even try to stop him, at least not until he wanted to stop. And where he stopped was at the gate leading to the little children's play area, with its brightly coloured swings and slides and tunnels and climbing frames. *Under-fives only*, said the notice.

"I'm sure Stone Croc's under five," said Meera.

"Who cares if he isn't," said Alice, opening the gate. "Why don't I fetch Mac? He's under five."

"Mac will tell everyone about it tomorrow," worried Meera. "Then where will we be?" She longed for Alice to fetch Mac now, all the same.

"So what?" argued Alice. "When he says he was in the park in the middle of the night with Stone Croc, Mum'll just think it's another of his stories."

Meera might have felt frightened then, when Alice had gone, all alone in

Ravenscourt Park in the moonlight. But of course she wasn't alone really. She had Stone Croc. And Stone Croc wanted to go on everything in the under-fives playground. No wonder, Meera thought, as she swung him on the swings, and pushed him down the slides. He must have been watching children play on swings and climbing frames ever since he was

brought to the park. She felt quite sorry for him, thinking of that, as Stone Croc came down the slide over and over, first on his back, then lying forwards on his belly. Afterwards he climbed the ladder up to the climbing frame and fell off.

"I could have told you crocs wouldn't be any good at climbing," said Meera, helping him on to a swing instead. A red one it was, but in the moonlight it looked the same colour as the blue one next to it, and only a bit darker than the yellow swing beyond that.

After a while Meera forgot she wasn't an under-five, even if Stone Croc was. Next time Stone Croc slid down the slide, she followed him. Then they both crawled through two of the tunnels. Then they both went on the swings again. Stone Croc's claws were hooked round the chains of the blue swing, Meera sat next door to him on the red one. She had swung herself as high as the little swing could go, when she saw Alice coming towards them across the grass holding a

sleepy-looking Mac in one hand and
carrying a large bag in the other.

"I brought us a picnic," she said.
"Crisps and frankfurters and tomatoes
and chocolate biscuits. Being out
at night makes me hungry.
Doesn't it you?"

"I don't know," said Meera. "I'm not used
to being out at night." As far as she knew
Alice wasn't used to being out at night either.
But she did not say so.

Mac didn't remain sleepy-looking for long. There were four different play places in the park and they went into three of them. Alice looked like a giant, Meera thought, perched up on a tiny slide in the little children's playground, or with her legs tucked beneath her on one of the low swings. She looked more normal-sized on the bigger slides and swings of the older children's place. But now Mac looked very small. Or maybe it was just the effect of the mysterious moon, making everything look different, thought Meera.

Finally, Stone Croc led them to the marvellous wooden gangways and contraptions of the adventure playground at the back of the park. Standing with your feet on either side of an iron foothold, on the end of a bar fixed by a pulley to a steel rope running between two towers, you could swing from one to the other and some way back again if you wanted. Even Meera had not been on that kind of swing before. Mac was too small to go on his own. He went

with Meera, standing in front of her, his feet on top of hers, both of them clinging to the iron bar. Alice went with Stone Croc. Who sat, sort of. That was the only way you could describe it, Meera thought. But she did not want to hurt him by laughing at him.

It did not matter. They were all so happy. It was hard to know which of them loved that game most.

"*Sssh*," said Meera, anxiously, "*Sssh*.

Someone will hear us if we're not careful."
For it was hard not to shout with delight
swinging out and back, the ground shifting
underneath them, the moon as if turning,
above their heads. They were all of them
laughing and calling to each other now.

"Again," said Mac. "Want it 'gain. Want it
'gain, Meera."

"So do I want it 'gain, Mac," said Alice.
"Just look at Stone Croc. He wants it 'gain
too."

"This is the best night of my whole life,"
said Meera. And so it was the best night of
her whole life. What did they matter, all those
years between Alice's fourteen years, her nine
and Mac's three. There they were, like any
family of brothers and sisters, two sisters, a
brother, their friend, swinging and jumping in
the moonlight, playing together, enjoying the
same things. If their friend was a stone
crocodile, so what? All they needed now was
for their dad to come home every night like a
proper dad, thought Meera.

There was one play place in the park they did not go to, of course; the enclosure with the paddling pool and the sandpit. When Mac said, "Want to paddle, now. Want to play in the sand," Alice said loudly, "Time for our picnic, Mac. Aren't you hungry?"

"Mac *very* hungry," said Mac.

Meera felt exhausted suddenly, as well as hungry. She was not the only one. Even before they had eaten all the crisps and frankfurters and tomatoes and chocolate biscuits, Mac fell asleep on the grass. So did Stone Croc. Alice sat cross-legged on the picnic table whistling to herself, while Meera lay on her back, between Mac sucking his thumb as he slept, and Stone Croc, whose stone belly she could only just feel going up and down. She looked up at the huge moon, at the sky glowing orange with the lights of the city and was happy.

"Wake up, Meera," she heard suddenly. "You're falling asleep. I think it's time we went home," said Alice.

Alice carried the still sleeping Mac. Meera coaxed Stone Croc along because he was too heavy for her to carry. Although he walked very slowly and heavily, he did not need much coaxing. Meera could see he knew just where he was going. She knew where he was going too. So did Alice. When they got to the fence that ran around the sandpit and paddling pool, they saw the two other bigger crocodiles lying there. Stone Croc standing at their feet looked no different; apart from being smaller.

"Do you want to go in, Stone Croc?" asked Alice.

"Listen to him; of course he does," said Meera. Stone Croc was making another of his rare noises; a series of little squeaks this time, which could have meant hello or goodbye, happiness at going home, sadness at saying goodbye. Most likely all those things. It didn't matter.

The gate was open, though it should have been shut. Meera waited till Stone Croc had

waddled inside, then closed it behind him with a little click. They could see all three crocodiles now, all silver grey by the light of the moon, the two bigger ones half buried in sand as usual. Stone Croc did not touch them as he passed. He just lay down beside them in his old place. At once it was as if he had never been away.

"Goodbye, Stone Croc," said Alice as she and Meera turned for home, walking very slowly and thoughtfully.

"Perhaps that was all he really wanted, all the time. Just to go on the swings and so on," said Meera.

"Wouldn't you have wanted to if you were him, sitting in the park the whole day long, watching everyone else doing it?" said Alice.

"That was what I thought," said Meera, sure it must be true if both she and Alice thought it.

They all missed Stone Croc. "Where's my Crockie?" Mrs Fisk kept asking. "What's happened to my Crockie?"

After a month or so, she came home one day with a kitten. "My new Kitty. So I won't be lonely any more," she said. "You can come and play with him sometimes, Mac, if you're a good boy and promise not to pull his tail."

Mac did pull the kitten's tail, of course. But the kitten did not stay around like Stone Croc, it went away and hid and wouldn't come out.

"Want Stone Croc," said Mac looking sad. "Of course you do, Mac," said Meera. Downstairs Mum's sewing machine clacked and purred, making covers with roses on, for a change. Outside the trains rattled along the track. "Let's go and find Stone Croc in the park," she said.

"Go find Stone Croc," said Mac.

They visited Stone Croc most days. So did a lot of other people. Stone Croc was famous for a while, for going away one day and coming back another. But only Meera and Alice and Mac knew where he'd been, and Meera and Alice, at least, weren't telling.

Mac played with Stone Croc just as he always had, piling sand on him, rolling on him, pulling his ears. Stone Croc lay as if sleeping once again, he did not move a single muscle. Or hardly a muscle, anyway. Once or twice, Meera could have sworn an eye opened and looked at her, then closed again.

"Hello, Stone Croc," she would whisper, and hurry Mac off to the swings or the paddling pool before he took a fancy to playing with one of the bigger sandpit crocodiles; before they, too, started winking at her, or, please no, rising to their feet. She still thought their teeth a bit too big.